little Miss Contrary

by Roger Hargreaves

PSS!
PRICE STERN SLOAN

Little Miss Contrary always did the opposite of what you would think she would do.

For instance:
if you asked her to switch on the television, she would switch on the light.

For example:
if you asked her the time, she would tell you the date.

And she always said the opposite of what she really meant!

Mind you.

It wasn't exactly her fault.

It was probably because she lived in a place called Muddleland where everything is so mixed up and muddled you don't know whether you are coming or going.

Or "going and coming" as they say in Muddleland.

It's a very strange place indeed!

The worms don't live in holes in Muddleland.

They live in trees!

And the birds live in holes!

And if you want a loaf of bread you don't go to the baker's, you go to the butcher's.

The baker sells bananas!

One morning, Little Miss Contrary
was having breakfast.

Roast beef and Yorkshire pudding.

There was a knock at the door.

Little Miss Contrary didn't hear it at first
because it was more of a tap than a knock.

Tap . . . tap . . . tap.

But she did hear it eventually,
and went to see who it was.

She opened the door.
"Hello," said a little voice.

Little Miss Contrary looked down,
and down again, and there stood Mr. Small.
He raised his hat. "Hello," he said again.

"Goodbye," smiled Little Miss Contrary.

Mr. Small looked puzzled. As well he might!
"I wonder if you can help me?" he asked.

Little Miss Contrary smiled.
"Of course I can't," she said.

"Oh dear," said Mr. Small. "You see, I'm lost!"

"Well," she said. "Nice to meet you, Mr. Lost!"

"No! No!" said Mr. Small. "I'm trying to find someone called Little Miss Contrary!"

"That's you," laughed Little Miss Contrary

"I have a letter for her," said Mr. Small.

"Oh bad," she said, "I don't get any telephone calls!"

"I think I'll go," said the confused Mr. Small. "Goodbye!"

"Hello," said Little Miss Contrary, and she shut the door.

Mr. Small went home, shaking his head.

The letter was from Mr. Happy, inviting Little Miss Contrary to his birthday party.

Mr. Happy had never met Little Miss Contrary, but he had heard about her, and thought it would be nice to have her at his party.

The invitation was for three o'clock on Tuesday the fourteenth of March.

At two o'clock on Monday the thirteenth of March,
Little Miss Contrary knocked on Mr. Happy's door.

"Merry Christmas," said Little Miss Contrary
and thrust a package into Mr. Happy's hands.

Mr. Happy was puzzled. "Who are you?" he asked.

"I'm Little Miss Sunshine," replied Little Miss Contrary.

"No you're not," said Mr. Happy.
"I know Little Miss Sunshine, and she's not
a bit like you."

Then he stopped and thought.

"Oh," he smiled. "I know who you really are.
You're Little Miss Contrary, aren't you?
I've heard you always say and do
the opposite of what you mean!"

"You'd better come in," said Mr. Happy.
"No thank you," smiled Little Miss Contrary.

Mr. Happy led her into his living room.
"What a horrible room," she said.
Mr. Happy grinned. He was beginning to realize
that everything he had heard about
Little Miss Contrary was true.

"Would you like a cup of tea?" he asked.
"I can't think of anything I'd like less,"
said Little Miss Contrary.
Mr. Happy grinned again, and went to put
the kettle on.

After his tea, Mr. Happy took Little Miss Contrary to meet some of his friends.

He had to explain to them all that what she was saying was the exact opposite of what she really meant.

"Aren't you thin?" she said to Mr. Greedy.

"You have very short arms!" she said to Mr. Tickle.

"I like your beard!" she said to Mr. Fussy.

"Well," she said eventually. "Thank you for the most perfect afternoon. Now I must go home before it gets light!"

"Perfect?" asked Mr. Happy.
"Perfectly dreadful," she agreed.
And off she went.

"I say," chuckled Mr. Greedy to Mr. Happy,
"you do know some funny people!"
"You can say that again," laughed Mr. Happy.
"You do know some funny people," said Mr. Greedy.
Mr. Happy grinned, and went home.

At home, Mr. Happy remembered the package
that Little Miss Contrary had given him.

"It must be a birthday present," he said.
And he hurried to where he had left the package,
and unwrapped it. Inside was indeed a present,
and a card. He opened the birthday card first.

Inside it said:
"MANY MISERABLE RETURNS OF THE DAY."

And, would you like to know what the
present was?

A pair of socks.

Well.

Not quite a PAIR of socks

One sock was white!

And the other sock was black!

And, as Little Miss Contrary would say, "that is the beginning of the story!"